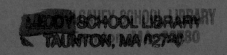

The Laziest Boy in the World

Lensey Namioka

The Laziest Boy
in the World

illustrated by YongSheng Xuan

Holiday House / New York

Many, many years ago there lived a Chinese boy called Xiaolong. He was the laziest boy in his village—maybe the laziest in the whole province. He may have been the laziest boy in all of China.

He was so lazy that he didn't cry or kick much even as a baby, because it was too much work.

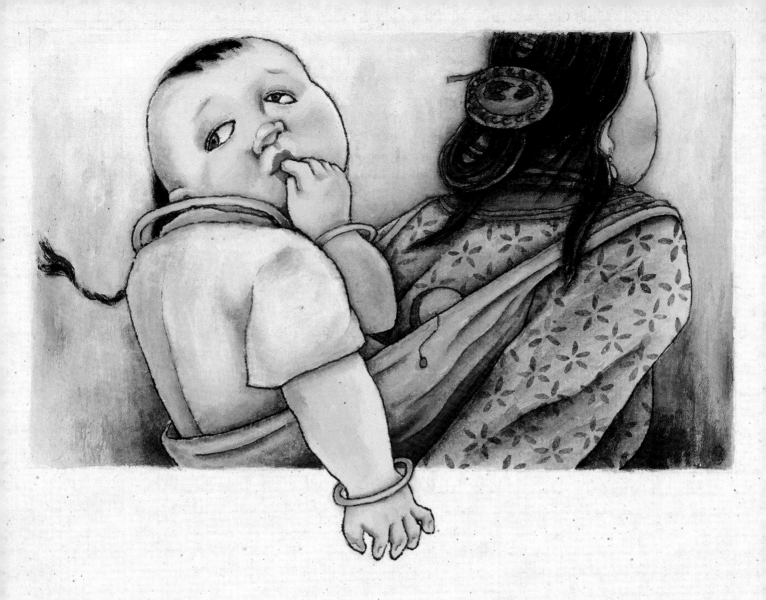

He was so lazy that even after he could walk, he still wanted his mother to carry him on her back. He couldn't get into
mischief this way, but getting into mischief was too much
work anyway.

He was so lazy that when his little chair tipped over one
day, he didn't try to get up. He just lay on his back, staring at
the ceiling.

At the age of three Xiaolong became old enough to eat with chopsticks, and he joined the rest of the family at the dinner table. When he was eating rice one day, he dropped a chopstick. Instead of picking it up, he began eating with a single stick. It was very slow work, but Xiaolong wasn't in a hurry. He was never in a hurry.

Xiaolong was the only son, the precious one who would carry on the family name. All the other children in the family were girls, who weren't supposed to count. Xiaolong's parents looked after him tenderly. They rushed to serve his every need and made sure he never had to wait for anything.

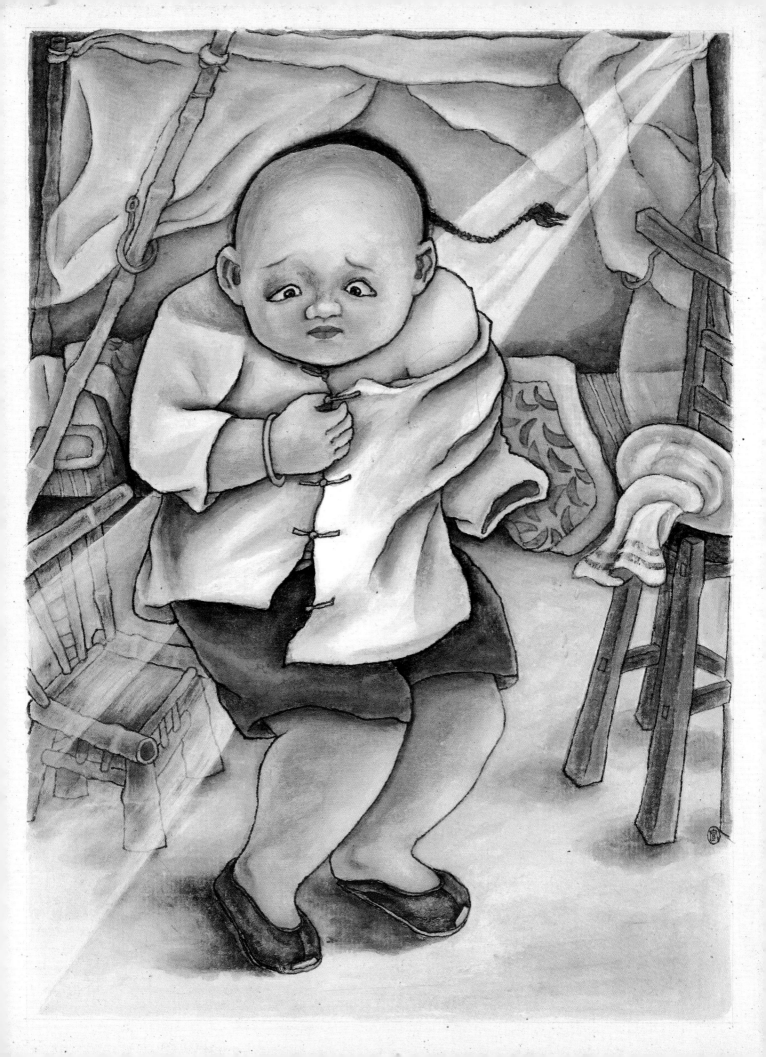

When Xiaolong reached the age of ten, his mother thought he was old enough to dress himself. Patiently, she taught him how to fasten the front of his jacket by pushing the buttons through their loops. Sometimes he made a mistake and pushed the first button into the second loop, the second button into the third loop, and so on down the line. This made the left side of the jacket higher than the right, but he didn't bother to do the buttons over again. The jacket stayed fastened, didn't it?

Slowly, very slowly, Xiaolong washed his face when he got up in the morning. He decided to wash the left side of his face one day, and the right side the next day, since it was too much work to wash his whole face. Often he didn't quite reach the middle, so there was usually a dirty stripe down the center of his face.

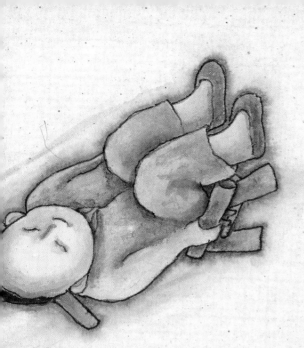

At an age when other children liked to run around outside to play, Xiaolong stayed inside and imagined himself playing games. He enjoyed kite flying best because he loved seeing the wind lift the kite up, up, up. Sitting in his little chair, watching his sisters fly the kite, he could almost feel its string tugging at his hands.

When he watched other children play tug of war, Xiaolong imagined himself on one team, pulling hard on the rope. If his side won, he cheered as loudly as the others on his team. Even if his side lost, Xiaolong didn't mind. He was a good loser.

Xiaolong's family were farmers, and his sisters worked in the fields with their father. Once his mother had to go out and help. Who would fix Xiaolong's meals while she was away?

Then she had an idea. "I'll make a big bread with a hole in the middle," she said. "I can hang it around your neck, and you can nibble on it all day."

So Xiaolong's mother rolled out dough, sprinkled salt and onions on it, folded it together, pressed it flat, and baked it on a pan. After the bread was cool, she cut a big hole in the middle and hung it around Xiaolong's neck.

"There!" she said, beaming. "That will keep you fed until I come back tonight."

But when she came home that evening, she saw that most of the bread was lying on the ground, still uneaten. Xiaolong was sitting on his chair, looking starved.

"Oh, my poor precious!" she cried. "Didn't you like the bread?"

"It was delicious," said Xiaolong. "But when I ate the front part, the bread broke and fell off my neck, so I couldn't get at the rest."

The family tried to think of a job for Xiaolong to do. His father finally had an idea: They owned a water buffalo for plowing their field and carrying loads. His son could become a buffalo herdsman and ride the animal around to graze when it wasn't working. This would be the perfect job for a boy who didn't move much.

During summer, the rice paddies were flooded so that the rice plants could stand in the water and grow faster. One day, while Xiaolong was riding the water buffalo, it began to graze near the paddies. It ate a clump of grass near a paddy, then it ate another clump, and another. Each time the buffalo stepped closer to the water.

Seeing the danger, Xiaolong pulled at the reins to get the buffalo away from the edge. He didn't have the energy to pull very hard, and the animal ignored his tugs.

Finally the buffalo noticed that it was at the very edge of the rice paddy. It stopped suddenly and stepped back. Xiaolong rolled off the buffalo and landed flat on his back in the muddy water.

The buffalo plodded away. Xiaolong lay in the warm mud and didn't bother to struggle up. It was much pleasanter just lying there, studying the sky. He would have spent the whole night in the paddy if his worried parents hadn't come searching for him.

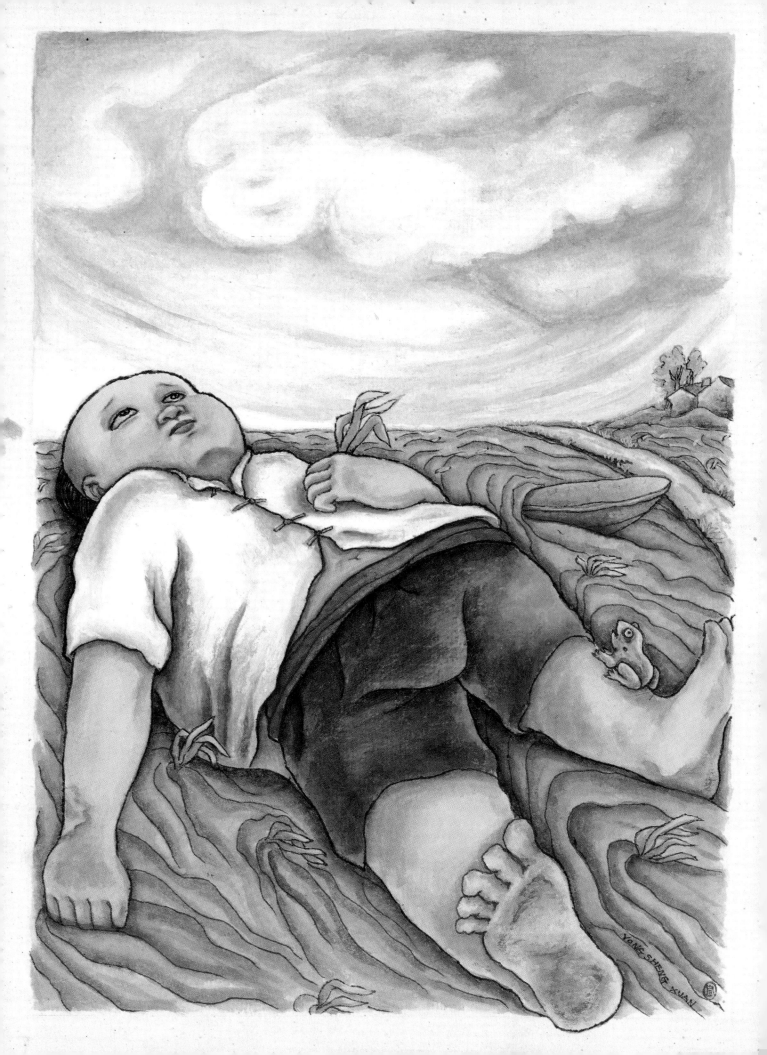

When Xiaolong wasn't riding the water buffalo, his favorite occupation was sitting in his chair by the window, looking at all the activities going on outside: He looked at his parents threshing the grain, at his sisters shooing away sparrows, at the neighbor's cat chasing the sparrows, and at their dog chasing the cat. Just by looking through the window, he could experience everything.

Then something happened that changed his whole life.

Late one night, a thief crept silently into the house. All the family was in bed, except Xiaolong. He had been gazing out at the stars and was so comfortable in his chair that he didn't bother to get up and go to bed.

The thief climbed in through the window and landed softly on the floor. He didn't see Xiaolong sitting in a dark corner.

Xiaolong was too frightened to make a sound. The thief crept around the room, putting things in his sack. He took some clothes, a cooking pan, and a bag of rice.

Xiaolong pictured his family the next morning, devastated by their loss. His mother, who adored him, would have to do without her cooking pan and supplies. His sisters, who told him nice stories and let him watch their games, would lose their clothes.

There was an unfamiliar burning sensation in Xiaolong's chest. It was anger. He didn't recognize it because he had never felt angry with anyone before.

I have to do something, Xiaolong told himself. But what? Anything he did would be dangerous and involve a lot of work.

Then he remembered that there was a pot of thick rice soup on the table left over from supper. Carefully and softly, he tiptoed over to the table, picked up the pot, and poured the soup quietly on the floor.

He returned to his chair, all worn out. He had never worked so hard before in his life.

When the thief finally decided there was nothing more worth stealing, he picked up his sack and started to leave. As he walked toward the open window, he skidded on the rice soup and fell, crashing into Xiaolong's chair. The two of them cracked their heads together, and they both cried out.

The noise woke up Xiaolong's family. His parents and sisters rushed into the room. They saw Xiaolong and the thief rolling around on the ground, and they hurriedly grabbed the thief, tied him up, and dragged him to the local magistrate's office.

When the news spread, everybody was astounded at Xiaolong's bravery and cleverness. His fellow villagers, who had thought he was just a useless lump, praised him lavishly and admitted they had done him an injustice.

Strangely enough, it wasn't the praise that Xiaolong enjoyed the most. It was something else.

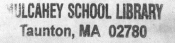

When Xiaolong walked across the room and poured the rice soup, the unaccustomed exercise had stretched his sinews and made the blood circulate faster in his muscles. Afterwards he had felt a funny ache and tingling in his limbs—and it was a rather pleasant sensation.

In the days that followed, he began to experiment. He would get up and walk a few tentative steps and even wave his arms gently. He discovered that he actually liked moving around!

His sisters noticed his activity. They decided that he was stronger than they had thought. Even his mother admitted that Xiaolong could move around when he wanted to.

Eventually his sisters and other young people invited Xiaolong to join their games, starting with the less strenuous ones.

One sunny, breezy day in early spring, Xiaolong stood outside on a gentle hill. His eldest sister, after running fast to get her kite soaring, came over to Xiaolong and handed him the string.

For the first time in his life, Xiaolong held a real kite string and felt it tugging at his hands. It was a wonderful moment. This was so much more fun than watching someone else fly the kite.

To the memory of my mother, who made
wonderful onion cakes!

L.N.

For my daughter, Faye Lee Xuan

Y.S.X.

The art is a combination of acrylic, watercolor, pen, and colored pencil.

Text copyright © 1998 by Lensey Namioka
Illustrations copyright © 1998 by YongSheng Xuan
All Rights Reserved
Printed in the United States of America
First Edition

Library of Congress Cataloging-in-Publication Data

Namioka, Lensey.
The laziest boy in the world / by Lensey Namioka;
illustrated by YongSheng Xuan. — 1st ed.
p.   cm.
Summary: When Xiaolong devises a way to capture the thief
who breaks into his family's home, all the people in the
Chinese village change their minds about the "lazy" boy.
ISBN 0-8234-1330-6
[1. Laziness—Fiction.   2. China—Fiction.] I. Xuan,
YongSheng, ill.   II. Title.
PZ7.N1426Laz 1998   [E]—dc21   97-9053   CIP   AC

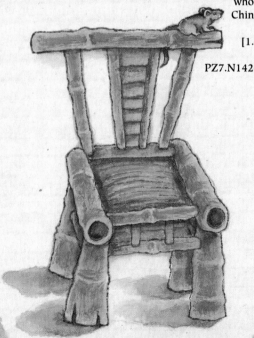